This igloo book belongs to:

..............................................

# igloobooks

Published in 2022
First published in the UK by Igloo Books Ltd
An imprint of Igloo Books Ltd
Cottage Farm, NN6 0BJ, UK
Owned by Bonnier Books
Sveavägen 56, Stockholm, Sweden
www.igloobooks.com

1122 002
2 4 6 8 10 9 7 5 3
ISBN 978-1-80022-673-9

Written by Stephanie Moss
Illustrated by Kathryn Inkson

Designed by Alice Dainty
Edited by Daisy Edwards

Printed and manufactured in China

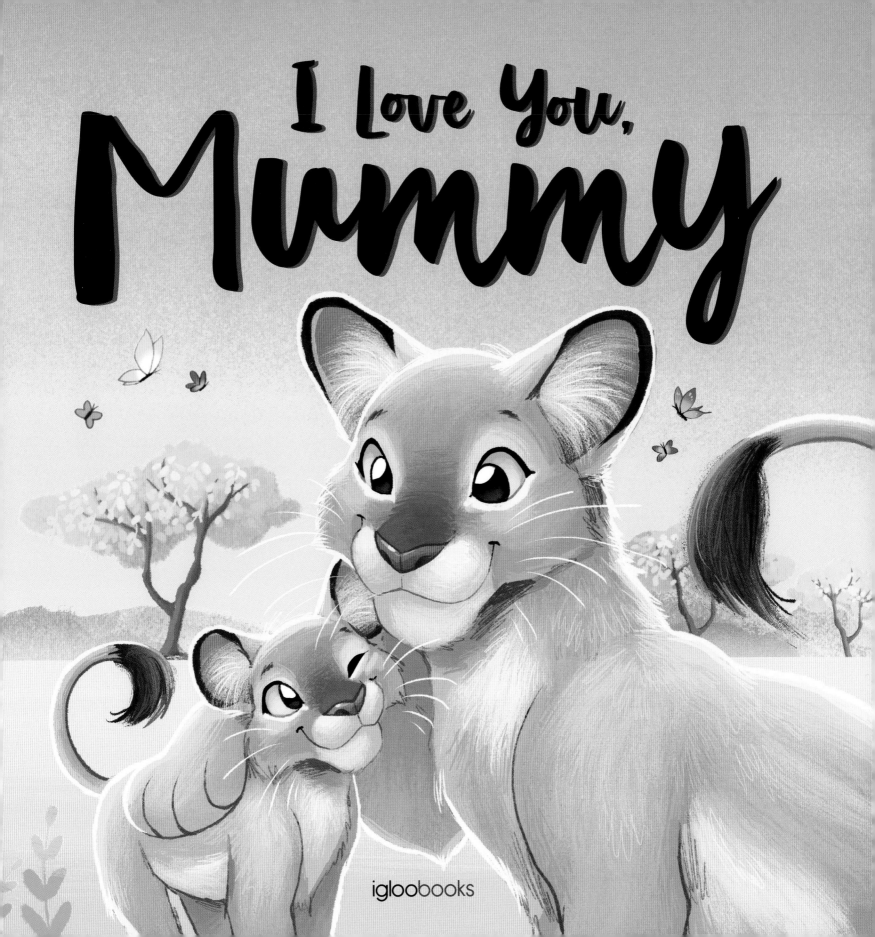

# I Love You, Mummy

igloobooks

Mummy, I love you.
Do you know how much?
Your kisses are kind,
with a soft, gentle touch.

You prowl and you pounce
so I know what to do.
One day, when I'm bigger,
I'll be just like you.

You say, "Let's be brave!"
when I curl up and hide.
Nothing's that scary
with you by my side.

Mummy, my hero.
You're fearless and wise.

For leading our family
you get the top prize!

I love you, Mummy.
You're snuggly and warm.
You've made me feel safe
since the day I was born.

We're tickly and giggly
and silly all day.

Mummy, I love the fun
games that we play.

If I fall on the ground or I'm stung by a bee, you make it feel better. You take care of me.

Mummy, I love making mischief together.
The muddiest, messiest memories ever!

When the sun's going down
and I feel like a rest,
cuddles with you are
the times I love best.

I snuggle beside you
and lay down my head.
You say, "Goodnight, little one.
Now, time for bed."